Arlo Bates

**Under the Beech Tree**

Arlo Bates

**Under the Beech Tree**

ISBN/EAN: 9783337423902

Printed in Europe, USA, Canada, Australia, Japan

Cover: Foto ©Andreas Hilbeck / pixelio.de

More available books at **www.hansebooks.com**

# UNDER THE BEECH-TREE
## BY ARLO BATES

BOSTON AND NEW YORK

HOUGHTON, MIFFLIN AND COMPANY

THE RIVERSIDE PRESS, CAMBRIDGE

1 8 9 9

TO THE MEMORY OF
ELEANOR PUTNAM

# CONTENTS

vii

# THE CHARGE

**W**HEN the day was at its dawn in golden
glory,
And the mist began to melt in mead-
ows low;
When the dream that all the night had told its
story
Followed darkness as it fled before the glow, —
Then we heard the warning bugle fiercely blow.

First a single gun rang out, the silence breaking,
And a hundred answered it with sudden crack;
Then our bugle shrieked alarm, in terror waking,
Till a trumpet from below cried the attack,
In defiance and derision shouting back.

So we waited not to wake, but still half dreaming
Got to saddle in the crispy morning air;
All the valley with the mists of night was steaming,
Thick with flashes flaming starlike here and
there,
And as light began to grow the flags shone fair.

I

Soft the light into the vale went slowly sinking,

Till we saw them file on file and rank on rank,

Thrice our number; and we set our teeth in think-
ing

How the sun on our dishonor last night sank,

And we burned to have them taste the cup we
drank!

And the word was cried at last: then, forward
leaping,

On we sprang our stolen honor to retrieve.

Did our comrades yester slain start in their sleeping,

Feel the pulse with which we thrilled, and long
to cleave

Through the sods with us this glory to achieve?

All the air was thick with shot, and shells were
shrieking

Their infernal cries of menace in our ear;

With the very fumes of hell the ground was reeking,

We were spattered with the blood of comrades
dear, —

But before us in the vale the foe showed clear!

Down the slope where with the frost the grass was
  shining,
  Past the brook set thick with rushes brown and
    tall ;
O'er the meadow, where the withered vines en-
    twining
  Caught the hoof, and made the reeling wounded
    fall,
  On we galloped, madly dashing over all.


Whence or how I cannot tell, so swiftly springing
  From the fog and from the smoke the close
    troop came,
But before us were the Guards, in gallop swinging
  As last night they bore us down, a sweeping
    flame,
  While their bugle to the heaven cried our shame.


How we shouted in mad joy of this fierce meet-
    ing !
  How with roweled heel we stabbed each horse's
    flank !
Slash of sabre was our welcome and our greet-
    ing,

3

As we hurled ourselves against them, rank to
rank,

And their eagled flag before us rose and sank.


All the murky air burned red before my vision,

Till I saw the leader close beside me wheel;

'T was De Vaux, his face a taunt of proud derision,

And I struck with all my soul to speed the steel.

God, what joy to see death-struck the traitor
reel!


As the scythe that hissing rushes through the
clover,

So we cut them to the earth in vengeance sweet;

How we broke and beat them down, and rode
them over,

As a stampede of wild cattle tread the wheat,

Till their pride was with their strength beneath
our feet.


There were few of us to hear the bugle calling

When that night the sun sank down into the
west;

On the graves of friend and foe the clods were
  falling, —
But we smiled upon our comrades there at rest
As we hugged our re-won honor to our breast!

# THE TRIUMPH OF SPRING

HEN, escaped from the dungeons where
Winter had bound her,
Fair Spring through the meadow and
woodland takes way,
What rejoicing, what jocund delight all around
her ;
What exuberant greetings make gladsome the
day !

Then the jubilant buds burst with joy of sweet
weather,
Breathing balsam and balm on the languorous
air ;
While the birds in the coverts go mating together,
Chirping eager of nests in the boughs lately
bare.

All the brooks brim, and babble with turbulent
laughter,
And gurgle and froth into quick glancing foam ;

Then the low cloudlets linger for winds which
come after
To whisper some hint of the pathways they
roam.

Then the violets troop, gay with youth's foolish
rapture,
To greet the blithe Spring in the path she must
pass ;
But they shrink like shy children, in fear lest foes
capture,
To cower and hide in the crystalline grass.

There the burly brown bumble-bee rifles their
kisses,
With his ardor amazing their innocence pure ;
There he breaks with rough riot their dream of
meek blisses,
And then flees from their weeping in boldness
secure.

Through the long, moonlit nights the first whip-
poorwill, plaining,
Pours its iterant sadness upon the soft air,

7

The repining of youth, half of truth and half
feigning,
That commingles love's joy with its torturing
care.


Oh, sweet madness of springtime! The seed that
sleeps darkling,
From the light of day hid in the bosom of earth,
Feels thy thrill, and outbursts to the sunlight's
warm sparkling,
By thy lure led along through the mazes of
birth.


Do the dead who lie lonely in slumber unwaking
Never tremble and shiver beneath spring's warm
beam?
Does no tremulous pulse-beat, trance passionless
breaking,
Stir their being at least with some dream of a
dream!

# A CORRESPONDENCE .

HIS LETTER

TOO long a lie that for itself usurped
   The name of love has stood between
      us.   Take
The truth at last, although it wring our souls,
Mine speaking as yours hearing.

                           Once our eyes,
Which cannot feign as ready lips may do,
Spoke deeply each to each, protesting love;
And I, thirsty for love, believed it won.
To-day our glances shifting turn aside,
Fearing to meet and let the truth be known.
How could you fail me so !   Ah, had it been
Myself that you had loved, — my very self,
Even with love so feeble as the spark
Of glow-worm drowned in dew, all had been well.
No palsied beggar with more grateful hand
Grasps a scant alms than I had eager stretched
For dole of love if you would have it so !
But you in me at best found never more
Than a clear mirror where yourself you saw,

Loving the image; counting not the glass.

No thought you had save that my heart was yours

To take or leave, to keep or throw aside;

I had no value save to make more clear

Your sweet perfection; had no worth apart

From that of being yours, — as canvas gets

By the great artist's touch so much of grace

That that which worthless was is priceless!   Bah!

You never for so brief a point of time

As the quick flutter of an eyelid loved,

Rating me for myself, a thing distinct

From your sweet condescension.

                              Let there be

An end!   I can no more endure to stand

The flattering mirror of your own self-love.

For me the perfect beauty of your face,

Your loveliness like that of dawn, your eyes

That once beguiled me with their sweet untruth,

Your hand whose touch once thrilled me so, no
        more

Have power or charm.   I am a man, and ask

That love be met with love.   I give no more

The passion of my life to feed your pride;

My heart to glut your vulture vanity!

We stand from hence apart, then.   No regret
Need trouble your smooth brow's complacency.
You lose no thing you valued.   You have loved
Nothing but self, and self remains to you.
I will go free !   You surely will not lack
Mirrors enough to do your beauty right.
If I find love at last, it shall be well ;
And if I find it not, — at least no more
A lie that trifles with the sacred name
Shall desecrate the chambers of my heart.
I wish you naught but happiness.   Farewell.


HER REPLY

" Too long a lie that for itself usurped
The name of love has stood between us.   Take
The truth at last."   And, O my friend, beware
Lest that truth, like a haftless knife, should cut
The hand which wields it.   You give bitter blows ; —
Blows such as some men strike at women's hearts, —
But is your palm unhurt ?
                              You say our eyes,
Which cannot feign, once spoke, protesting love.
Was it my glance that faltered on that day
When first a shadow came between ?   If now

11

My look turn back abashed before the truth,

It is not shame, but sorrow, blinds my sight.

I would not see that which you cannot hide.


My friend, my lover once, since you at last

Throw off allegiance, and "go free" — your
            word ! —

From chains grown irksome, I have now no fear

To ask what meant the protests numberless

Wherewith you swore you had no wish to be

Aught save what I would have ; no thought of life

Save as it ministered to my delight ;

That in return you asked no smallest boon

Save that you be allowed to love.

                        My friend,

Long has the day been passed when I believed

Such words as these ; but since not once you swore

These eager vows, but had them on the lip

Day after day, how can you count it then

A fault in me if I had faith, and took

The lover at his word ?   Dare you complain ?

Complaint is but confession you 're forsworn !

Truth is an ugly hag, and I forbear

To force her to your close embrace ; but yet

Must I say one poor word to ease my heart,

My foolish woman's heart, which aches to lose

What it confesses is not love.  We keep

The dust that was a rose, and lose with tears

Its shriveled mockery of bloom.

                                 What gave

Such quickness to your eyes to see in me

Vanity vulture-beaked?  Is love so keen

To spy the hidden blemish?  Can it be

That love was not your quest; that had I kneeled

In adoration rapt, I had been found

Still worthy of your favor?  Can it be

That somewhere through your armor-joints a shaft,

Chance-sent, hath hurt your pride; and you, amazed,

Discover this to be what you called love?


I loved you, — or I loved the man I thought

Was you; and chillingly day after day

You thrust upon me proof and proof again

That what you are is to the thing I loved

As shadow is to substance.  Do you think

A woman loves, and finds herself deceived

In him she loves, finds his soul small and mean

Which she had thought a glorious expanse

Where she might stretch her wings and upward

  ,    soar,

Finds him she counted strong weaker than she,

Finds her ideal lost, yet suffers not?

Deep in her bosom aches the rankling sting

Of keen humiliation, — part for self,

But more for him she loved.   Far better death

Than disenchantment!   Then —

                              But let it be.

What boots it to pile words on words when love

Is done, and done forever?   Go your way.

Find what you take for love, and cherish it.

Be happy if you can.   I love you not;

And yet I would have died — I still could die, —

For love of that which once I thought was you!

14

## TO THE FELLOW IN THE COCK-LOFT
## OF MY BRAIN

OLD fellow in my brain's top attic,
'T is both pathetic and dramatic
    That you with sad, grief-haunted eyes
  Sit ever striving to devise
  For me to say, things gay or wise.


Ofttimes if these win praise or laughter
Almost a sob will choke me after,
    As I remember how in pain
  You sit there lonely in my brain,
  Shaping these fancies rich or vain.


Your untouched loneliness appalls me ;
Yet would I share it this befalls me, —
    To find your door closed in my face.
  I even am denied the grace
  Low at your feet to take my place.


But ah, the songs I hear you singing, —
In tongues I do not know out-ringing

Clear to the stars; so deadly sweet

That hardly can my crushed heart beat,

And I with tears could kiss your feet.

Could I repeat those measures burning,

Those lays which speak immortal yearning,

Then would men all their woes forget,

Their eyes with tears of joy be wet,

Each dear, dead hope spring living yet!

I know not what deep secret, reaching

Beyond man's ken, those lays are teaching;

But would I sing them, my poor tongue

Falters and fails, and leaves unsung

The heavenly strain hath my heart wrung.

Is it for this that you have flouted

My best endeavors, till I doubted

The worth of all I do or dream,

Seeing the things I precious deem

Could win from you but scorn supreme?

Yet in despite of all, I love you!

Much I lament that fate above you

Hath fixed so firm its stern decree —

Or your own whimsy can it be ? —

That you should care no fig for me.

Why so unwilling I should know you ?

'T is naught but kindness I would show you.

When did I e'er against you sin ?

Since I so long your love to win

Why will you keep your latch-string in ?

17

# RANTING ROBIN

Kenilworth, I.

HEN ranting Robin of Drysandford
    went to the siege of the Brill,
    Not a blither lad or a bolder blade
  To fight in the trenches or woo a maid
      Could England boast ;
      And he was our toast,
  Sturdy and stalwart still.

But ranting Robin of Drysandford, there at the
    siege of the Brill,
  Met his death in a ditch with his sword in hand ;
  And the bravest bully in all our band
      Lay dead, alack !
      When we turned back, —
  Death had of him its will.

Sweet ranting Robin of Drysandford, before the
    siege of the Brill
  How many a night till the gray dawn's crack

Have we made good cheer, have we burned good
sack.
What songs we sang
Till the rafters rang
With shoutings hoarse or shrill.


Hot ranting Robin of Drysandford, how at the
siege of the Brill
Didst thou swagger and bluster with ready
blade
Would leap from its scabbard all undismayed
By foes a score.
Alas! no more
Thy sword red blood will spill.


Gay ranting Robin of Drysandford, cursed be the
siege of the Brill!
Where thy bold heart stopped, and thy strong
blade fell,
And thy roystering tongue that we loved so well
Was stilled in death.
For ne'er drew breath
Comrade we spared so ill!

Bold ranting Robin of Drysandford, dead at the

siege of the Brill!

May thy sleep be sweet, and thy ghost have rest,

By lack nor of sack nor of love oppressed!

Whenever we drink

Our beakers we'll clink,

And toast thy memory still.

## TO A FADED ROSE

POOR rose, you so lately were fair,
But now, all your pink petals blight-
ed,
You drop from her dark, perfumed hair
To fall quite forgotten and slighted.

Pathetic and withered you lie;
Yet need is there none I should mourn you :
Neglected and faded you die, —
But ah, happy rose, she has worn you!

# FULFILLED DESIRE

IF one love love and one love fame,
 Desire of both may fail;
If one love life, as fades a flame
 Full soon life's lip grows pale.

But who loves death need only wait,
 Unmoved by doubt or fear;
Secure that every moment fate
 Brings his desire more near.

# CONCEITS

## I. KITTY'S LAUGH

THY laugh 's a song an oriole trilled,
    Romping in glee the sky, —
Sunshine in lucent drops distilled,
    And showered from on high.

So perfect in his song thou art,
    That when thy laughter rings
I long to clasp thee to my heart,
    Lest too thou have his wings !

## II. KITTY'S "NO"

Kit, the recording angel wrote
    That cruel "no" you said ;
And smiled to think how in your throat
    You choked a "yes" instead ;

Then sighed in envy of the look
    That promised me your grace ;
And on the margin of his book
    Limned in excuse your face.

III. A LOVER'S FEAR

To fetch your fan I was sent,
  Which you 'd left in the room behind you.
Terror seized on my heart as I went,
  And I wondered if I should find you
Alive and well and the same,
When back with the fan I came!


IV. AN AUBADO FOR KITTY

I wove a web of dreams, like cobweb-net
  In jasmine thickets full of golden bloom,
Which snares at midnight, when the moon is set,
    The great night-moth, that up and down the
    gloom
  On pale blue wings sails drunken with perfume.


I thought to snare a vision of thy face
  To bless my sleep ; but all the night forlorn,
Restless and lone I slumbered in my place.
  Empty my futile web until the morn ;
  Even my dreams won naught but mocking scorn.


But as the web among the jasmine spread
  Glittering with dew in morning light appears,

24

Torn where the noxious beetles hurtling shred,
My snare hung tattered by night-haunting fears,
And every filmy mesh was starred with tears.

V.  A DEDICATION

I send thee, Kitty dear, my book ;
'T is full of thoughts of thee.
Oh, bless it with that tender look
Thou hast denied to me.

The myrrh-tree, wounded, proffers gum ;
The poet's heart, its song ;
Sweet, so my verses to thee come
Because thou dost me wrong.

And yet if thus I harshness pay,
When shall I kindness see ?
The more thou dost approve the lay,
The crueler thou 'lt be !

25

# ADMONITION

UP, and be doing, for the night draws near
   Wherein no man can work! Live in
   to-day,
And so live for eternity. For here
   And now thy moment is, — but will not stay.


He who lives in to-day with hearty zest
   Best for the future lives. Be not afraid
To give thine all upon to-day's behest,
   And face a bankrupt future undismayed.


Be spendthrift of thy soul if good the cause ; —
   And losing find that thou hast gained the whole.
Miss not the race for one faint-hearted pause ;
   Think not of breath till thou hast gained the
   goal!


To-day is now, and now the future is, —
   Within thy clasp if so it be thy will ;
Who grasps to-day, the whole of time is his ;
   Future and past the present holdeth still.

# BABY THEODORE

WHAT though the sun forget to shine?
  There 's Theodore!
What though the wailing wind repine?
  Here 's Theodore!
Though wind and rain and sky should fret,
The sun becloud his face, we yet
The gloom of nature may forget
  With Theodore.


There is no sunlight like the smiles
  Of Theodore;
He weaves a net of golden wiles,
  Sly Theodore!
No dove hath softer voice to coo,
No fay more witchingly could woo;
And even poetry's praise is true
  Of Theodore!

27

# THE JUDGMENT DAY

WHEN the Judgment Day is come,
   Not from His throne supernal
   Shall God to souls struck dumb
   Mete woe or bliss eternal.

Then the soul itself alone
   Shall doom beyond appealing;
How each to self is known
   In awful truth revealing.

28

# IN PARADISE

"PITYING angel, pause, and say
   To me, new come to Paradise,
   How I may drive one pain away
By penitence or sacrifice.
From deeps below of nether Hell
   I hear a lost soul's bitter cry;
Alas!   It was through me she fell, —
   What price forgetfulness may buy?"

The passing angel paused in flight,
   Poised like fair stars which first arise,
And looked on that pale suppliant white,
   With piercing pity in his eyes.
"Ah, woe!" he said.   "Thy joy and peace
   Cannot be bought with prayer or price.
For thee that wail will never cease,
   Though thou hast won to Paradise!"

# THE CYCLAMEN

VER the plains where Persian hosts
   Laid down their lives for glory
   Flutter the cyclamens, like ghosts
  That witness to their story.
Oh, fair!  Oh, white!  Oh, pure as snow!
On countless graves how sweet they grow!

Or crimson, like the cruel wounds
  From which the life-blood, flowing,
Poured out where now on grassy mounds
  The low, soft winds are blowing;
Oh, fair!  Oh, red!  Like blood of slain;
Not even time can cleanse that stain.

But when my dear these blossoms holds,
  All loveliness her dower,
All woe and joy the past enfolds
  In her find fullest flower.
Oh, fair!  Oh, pure!  Oh, white and red!
If she but live, what are the dead!

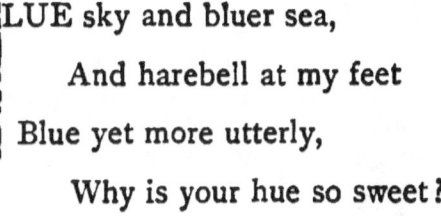LUE sky and bluer sea,
  And harebell at my feet
Blue yet more utterly,
  Why is your hue so sweet?

What fibre of my soul
  Thrills at your loveliness?
Why should a tint control
  My heart like a caress?

Blue sky and bluer sea
  And harebell at my feet,
How can mere color be
  Beyond all telling sweet?

# THE GIFT

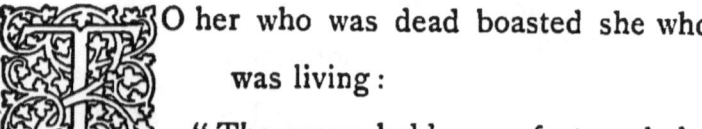T O her who was dead boasted she who
    was living:
  "The grave holds you fast, and de-
    vours your charms;
The love that was yours unto me he is giving.
  Forgotten you lie, while he laughs in my arms."


But she who was dead answered her who was
  living:
  "Your soul knows your lie though your boasting
    is brave.
That which he has given is not for his giving.
  His heart is still mine, beating warm in my
    grave!"

# THOU, ONLY THOU

THOU, only thou within my heart canst
    reign ;
  Thou, only thou, although a god should
    deign
To stoop from heaven thy place to claim, and be
Incarnate rapture brooding over me.
    Thou, only thou !


Thou, only thou, although an hour spanned
Thy term of life, and I alone must stand
Through all eternity.　More that brief grace
Than ages with another in thy place.
    Thou, only thou !


Thou, only thou, since I must cease to be
All that I am to cease from loving thee.
Not Paradise could bribe me from thy grave ;
Thou art the immortality I crave ; —
    Thou, only thou !

# THE STORM-WIND

STORM – WIND of the mountain, speeding fleet
From cloud-washed peak to cloud-washed peak! How free
And strong and terrible thou art! The sea
Bred thee in her vast womb, the offspring meet
Of her supreme espousals with the heat
    And passion of the sky. Thy sire to thee
    Gave as thy dower all power, that thou shouldst be
Monarch and lord where'er thy fierce wings beat.

The forests at thy feet fall down in fear;
    The fair frail mist-shapes cower in awful dread,
Or shivering flee thy trumpet tones to hear;
But thou goest on unstayed, as God's voice sped
    Down chaos at the first, and sphere on sphere
The rolling worlds to ordered being led.

O wind implacable and stern as fate,

Thou art the messenger of God, to cry

The coursing of His chariot down the sky,

His coming sure for which the ages wait.

Rush on thy course like His consuming hate !

Be like His flame omnipotent, and fly

To make earth ready for His drawing nigh,

In glory measureless and uncreate.


Speed on thy way ineffable and grand !

Be as the breath of God himself to purge

From all uncleanness.   Let no foul thing stand

Affronting day !   Sweep with resistless surge ;

And with thy mighty besom cleanse the land,

Till thy triumphant cry is evil's dirge !

# MISNAMED

HOW many things men have misnamëd
    love : —
    Frail fancies light as cobweb-films in
    air,
The greed of thick-lipped lust, sweetness of dove
    And falcon fierceness, — things both foul and
      fair ;
The summer liking of a moment, caught
    Like thistle-down upon a minstrel's coat
And blown away by the same breeze that brought,
    No more remembered than a fallen mote ;
The insatiate fire of the selfish heart,
    Which feeds on homage as flame feeds on straw ;
The boundless insolence of pride, with art
    Fresh triumphs from affection's gifts to draw ; —

These they name love who cannot understand
Love is a mighty deep, unplumbed, unspanned !

36

# THE MAGDALENE

WOMAN, with the tresses of thine hair
For silken napkin, wipe those blessed
feet ;
Perfume them with thy spikenard ointment sweet,
And on them press thy lips, rose-petals fair ;
Lave them with thy hot tears in mute despair.
Prostrate and pale, passionately entreat
Forgiveness for thy sin and shame unmeet,
Till all thy soul dissolve in wordless prayer.

Yet, O sad sinner, no remorse avails
To change the guilty past.  Thy brow bears stain
From berries of shame's garland ; where that trails
It leaves its mark forever.  Not disdain
Wakes at thy grief ; yet thy petition fails : —
Thy brow's lost whiteness thou must weep in vain.

# THE CONQUERED

E who so eager started on life's race,
And breathless ran, nor stinted any
whit
For aching muscles, or the parching grit
Of dust upon the lips ; who set the face
Only more desperately toward the place
Where the goal's altar smoked, if runners knit
With stronger limbs out-ran us ; we who sit
Beaten at last ; — for us what gift or grace ?


Though we have been out-stripped, yet known
have we
The joy of contest ; we have felt hot life
Throb in our veins, a tingling ecstasy. —
The prize is not the wreath with envy rife,
But to have been all that our souls might be.
Our guerdon is the passion of that strife !

## THE POOL OF SLEEP

 DRAGGED my body to the pool of
sleep,

Longing to drink ; but ere my throbbing lip

From the cool flood one Dives-drop might sip,

The wave sank fluctuant to some unknown deep.

With aching eyes that could not even weep,

    I saw the dark, deluding water slip,

    Slow eddying, down ; the weeds and mosses drip

With maddening waste. I watched the sweet tide
creep

A little higher, but to fall more fast.

    Fevered and wounded in the strife of men

I burned with anguish, till, endurance past,

    The fount crept upward ; sank, and rose again, —

Swelled slowly, slowly, slowly, — till at last

    My seared lips met the soothing wave, and
then . . .

# THE ACCOUNT

WHEN in the sleepless watches of the night
I cast account with Fate, and set the ill
Against the good of life, then Fortune's slight
　Seems in remembrance yet more bitter still.
Then I recall how hopes have led me on —
　Will-o'-the-wisps that over quagmires play; —
How treacherous Joy has fled as soon as won,
　And hooded Sorrow darkling dogged my way;
How quickly into bitter turned the sweet;
　How swiftly clouds have dimmed heaven's blue;
How that which seemed most fair has been most
　　fleet,
　And that has proved most false which looked
　　most true.

But when against all this thy love I set,
I find myself Fate's bankrupt debtor yet!

# A REFLECTION ON FAME

TIME, whose cold touch tries all things,
    great and small,
  Shall prove my work if it be good or
    ill ;
Crumbled to dust disdainful let it fall,
  Or set it with the stars to glimmer still.
To me it will not matter, there in dust
  Drenched in dull sleep beyond the prick of
    dreams :
The dead no more for futile praises lust,
  No longer rage at cruel fate's extremes.
For fame is but a fevered, fitful breath,
  Infectious oft of ill, and stirring not
Even the grass upon the mound of death
  To rustle fleeting hints of things forgot.

And yet perchance the grave in which I lie
May bloom more fresh if that light wind pass by !

# THE GOLDEN AGE

# THE GOLDEN AGE

DREAM for a little.   Let the centuries
Crumble to dust like the light motes
that sift
Through sunbeams piercing to some dusky room
Which life has long forgot.   Seem not to be
Here in to-day, — to-day that doles out joy
In grudging drops ; that reckons beauty's worth
By what it earns of wage ; not in to-day,
But in some far, new time, — some golden age
Returned again, when love and hope and joy
And beauty bless once more the hearts of men :
When the old faith makes once again to smoke
The incense on the altars of the gods ;
And on men's lips the taste of life is sweet.

As if in dreaming, let your vision see
A softly rounded hill breathing of morn ;
The dew-drops not all dry, but glittering
With happy sparkles ; the thick violets

Melting in shadow as a languorous cloud

Softly floats over; while a bird unseen

Trills flutingly the bliss of life and love.

Below the wide, cool meadows, and the gray

Of olive groves, caught in the silver net

Of interlacing brooks.

                In such a scene

Move with our actors; play your part with them;

And for a little count the dream as true.


SCENE I

*Enter* STREPHON *and* PHAON, *bringing in a tripod.*

   *Strephon.* This is the place, here where the low
      hill spreads

A gracious greensward for the solemn rite;

And whence afar, a white gleam in the grove

Of olives, Daphne's house is seen.

   *Phaon.*                The house

Where Phœbe, when she woke two hours agone,

Sighed in remembering what to-day might bring,

Bewildered by the doubt as if not yet

She were awake.

   *Strephon.*     There is no doubt!

I tell you, Phaon, that it is as sure

As that the bud of night will bloom to morn

That Daphne's heart by riches will be bought,

And Phœbe's lovely self be mine.

    *Phaon.*                     Take care ;

Set not the tripod so far to that side.

    *Strephon.* Oh, you 'll not answer ! Will you own, at least,

Your wager lost ?

    *Phaon.*          My wager lost ! Ye gods,

How dull you are ! You wagered Phœbe's hand —

    *Strephon.* With her consent !

    *Phaon.*           With her consent of course :

How could you wager that which is not yours

Save by its owner's leave ?

    *Strephon.*             I wagered, then,

That Daphne weds with old Ægidius, rich —

    *Phaon.* And curst ! While I, whose love for Phoebe burns

With flame which is to yours as torch to spark,

Have set my happiness upon —

    *Strephon.*             The chance !

    *Phaon.* Not so ; upon the assurance doubly sure

That Daphne weds with Creon. Think you, boy,

         *Enter* PHŒBE *behind.*

47

I would have chanced my Phœbe's lightest breath,

Her footstep on the sand, her eyelash dropped,

Her —

   *Phœbe.* Well, her anything that's yours, belike !

   *Strephon.* Hail, Mistress Phoebe, mine so soon

      to be !

   *Phœbe. If* soon to be !

   *Phaon.*            Nay, since this day decides

There is no need to wrangle. Here to-day,

After the solemn sacrifice that crowns

The year's high prime, the summer's longest day,

Must Daphne give decision.

   *Phœbe.*            Yea, in sooth ;

And I, poor fool, teased by your bickering,

Intent to prove my faith that Daphne's heart

Is not an apple in the market-place

That may be bought, have set my fate on hers.

She chooses for herself and me. My hand,

A shadow to her substance, goes as hers.

   *Strephon.* That shadow to command, be I the

      sun !

   *Phaon.* May I but in that shadow ever dwell !

   *Phœbe.* Thanks for your wishes. As your na-

      tures are

So are your words.　But peace ; my mistress comes.

Let us go capture romping daffodils

And all the frolic blooms that flock the field ;

We shall want flowers against the feast to-night.

[*Exeunt omnes.*

SCENE II

*Enter* DAPHNE, ÆGIDIUS, *and* CREON.

*Ægidius.*　See ; all is ready for the solemn rite ;

The day is come : then, dearest Daphne, speak.

Say who shall own thy precious hand, whose touch,

Like that of Midas, turns all things to gold.

*Daphne.*　Nay ; not until the sacrifice is done

Must I proclaim my choice.　Till then as free

As the soft wind that hurries here and there

To steal the perfume from the asphodels

I hold my maiden heart.　But tell to me,

While yet my hand is still mine own to give,

By what ye rate my love.　First, Creon, thou.

　　*Creon.*　I love thee more than summer's golden

　　　　morn

When light begins to grow, and amorous birds

In every misty dell call to the sun

To hasten, that thy beauty may be seen.

49

I love thee more than even cool, wide night,

When all the winds have fled across the sea,

Enforcëd by the sun to follow him

And sing thy praises while he lacks thy smile ;

While the moon, envy-pale, steals through the sky

To spy on thee asleep !   I love thee more —

   *Ægidius.*   Nay, pile not foolish words !  If morns

      were gold,

They might with Daphne's loveliness compare.

Were the round moon one pearl, it might be held

A toy for Daphne's dower.   But for birds,

And winds, and all things pauper nature hath,

I rate them not ; and will not ye declare

Her worth by them.

   *Daphne.*              Good sir, then let us hear

What is the measure of thy love for me ?

   *Ægidius.*  I love thee more than rubies in whose

      depth

Burns the red, nimble fire untamable ;

Than the broad topaz, yellow as the eyes

The sleepy tiger blinks in coverts dusk ;

Than the quick opal, swarming full of flames

That mock the changing, iridescent hues

Which in keen polar nights th' aurora shows.

*Daphne.* Your words proclaim your minds.   I
have to choose

Between who rates all things by worth of gold

And him who counts up things intangible.

Thy treasure, O Ægidius, may be felt,

And weighed, and counted.   Creon, as for thine,

Thy gold is in the sunshine, and thy gems

Are dew-drops glinting on the weeping rose

That mourns her penury.   I will reflect.

Let us go in.   After the sacrifice

The gods my vow shall hear and register.

> [*Exeunt,* ÆGIDIUS *leading* DAPHNE.


SCENE III

*Enter* PHAON *and* STREPHON *with coals for the
tripod.*

*Strephon.* I say that old Ægidius had her hand,

And that he smirked with eager lips a-twitch,

And greedy eyes that gleamed with frosty light

To see the prize in reach.

*Phaon.*                    While Creon walked

With face downcast, and look of very woe.

*Strephon.* Ha!   Saw you that?   Then own your

wager lost.

*Phaon.* When it is lost! The crag that seems
to fall

May yet outlast the centuries.

*Enter* PHŒBE.

*Phœbe.* Saw ye
Ægidius lead my mistress down the hill,

While Creon followed after woeful pale

As he were hope's chief mourner?

*Strephon.* Said I not
It would be so! Now, Phœbe, art thou mine;

Come, girl, and kiss thy lord!

*Phaon.* Hold off your hand!
This hill shall be a place of sacrifice

To the infernal gods, if your rude lips

Brush bloom from cheek of hers!

*Phœbe.* My kisses yet
Are mine to give or keep; and, Strephon, thou

Shalt win them only as a gift from fate!

Think not that love will ever set my lips to
thine!

*Strephon.* Sayst thou so, mistress? Well, the
stars to-night

Shall greet thee as my bride. I am content.

*Phaon.* Hug to your bosom that content! Mayhap

'T will solace you when lonely nights are long!

*Phœbe.* Think'st thou that Creon's heart will

fail him now?

*Phaon.* Creon? Not he! He is of sterner stuff.

New-made high-priest, he bears upon his brow

The crown of manhood no less than the wreath

Of his great office.

*Strephon.* Hark! I hear the flutes.

Come, let us to our places.

[*Exeunt* STREPHON *and* PHAON.

*Phœbe.* O ye gods,

Let Daphne choose her husband with my eyes;

For my fate too upon that choosing lies!

[*Exit.*

SCENE IV

*Enter flute-players;* STREPHON *and* PHAON *bearing*
*flowers and incense;* CREON *in sacrificial robes;*
DAPHNE, ÆGIDIUS, *and* PHŒBE. *They circle*
*the tripod, strewing flowers, then* CREON *takes*
*his place beside it.*

*Creon.* With what rite, with what gift, with what

vow,

With what song, O divinest Apollo,

Shall we sue thee, and woo thee, that now,

As of old from thy Delphian hollow,

Thou wilt speak of high, hid things, and pour

A madness divine and compelling?

On what wings shall our pleading upsoar?

What hymn shall we waft to thy dwelling?

With what garlands, what incense, what wine,

With what dances in forest-set places,

With what baring of bosoms divine,

What uplifting of tremulous faces,

So entreat thee, so greet thee, that fleet

Down the cloud-way beneath thy steps glowing,

Thou wilt haste with beneficent feet,

Thy grace and thy presence bestowing?

Come, oh, come !

(STREPHON *throws on incense ; the flutes sound.*)

*All.* 	Come, oh, come !

*Creon.* 	Come, come, O most good, O most great !

Pierce our eyes with the glory of seeing ;

Teach our ears so to hear that, elate,

We shall learn the deep secrets of being.

Come, come, O most great, O most good !

Teach our hearts the true knowledge abiding

In the dusky green glooms of the wood,

   Where the nymph and the satyr are hiding ;

In the infinite yearnings that breathe

   Through the wind-hushes murmurous with mean-

      ing ;

In the odors of wild vines which wreathe

   Round the oak-bark the romp dryad screening ;

O thou god of the real and the true,

   Like a star from Olympus descending,

Let thy chariot flash out from the blue

   Of the deep heavens over us bending !

         Come, oh come !

(PHAON *throws on incense ; the flutes sound.*)

*All.*        Come, oh come !

*Creon.*  Oh, come down to us, golden Apollo !

         Come, oh come !

Let the Nine in their radiance follow.

Greatest Apollo, let our pleading reach thee ;

For with eyes wet and hearts full we beseech thee,

         Come, oh come !

Come like a flame in splendor earthward falling ;

Beneficent, have pity on our calling ;

         Come, oh come !

(CREON *throws on incense ; the flutes sound.*)

*All.*              Come, oh come !

[*The flutes begin again ; they encircle the altar,
    and exeunt.*

SCENE V

*Enter* PHAON *and* STREPHON.

*Phaon.* How can you doubt the issue ? Daphne's
    love
Is surely Creon's.

*Strephon.*          Well, and what is love ?
A little transient flame that flares and dies ;
An hour of sun before a tedious frost ;
The madness of a moment that begets
A bitter saneness after ; surfeit brief
Of honey cloying even as we taste !
Love is the fleeting paradise of fools !
But gold buys all ; buys even love, forsooth ;
Conquers the world, and makes man lord of fate !

*Phaon.* Peace !  Dare not on Apollo's sacred
    hill
Blaspheme at love to which the very gods
Are subject !  Gold may buy all things of earth ;
But love is the divinest gift of heaven.
Not in the market-places is it sold,

Or by swart mariners brought from far isles.

As the supremest gift of Heaven's grace
It kindles in the breast; and gold to love
Is as the dust beneath a maiden's feet
To her warm breath of life!

 *Strephon.*       Well, fool, prate on;
Bewilder life with dreams, and wake at last
To the benumbing coldness of the real!

 *Phaon.* Nay, I'll waste no more words. This
  hour will prove.
Come, let us hasten, or they will return.

 *Strephon.* Nay, why should I be slow, when bliss
  so fast
Speeds on to bless me that in her own robe
She trips, the jade!

 *Phaon.*      And should she trip indeed,
So that she fail to come, you'll call her jade
In quite another tone!

 *Strephon.*      Nay, never fear;
I feel assurance that she draweth near.

      (*They carry out the tripod.*)

SCENE VI

*Enter* DAPHNE *and* PHŒBE, *meeting.*

*Phœbe.*   O Mistress Daphne, from the sacrifice

A second time adown this fatal hill

I saw Ægidius lead thee by the hand.

Ah, whither hast thou been ?   What has he said !

His swelling port, and his old eyes aflame

Like cinders half burned out —

*Daphne.*                              Nay, saucy girl,

Rail not at good Ægidius !   He may be

Thy master ere thou art aware.   He led

Adown the hillside to the brook below,

And set me on the marge.   About my feet

The saffron primrose and forget-me-nots

As blue as if the pale reflected sky

Had tinged their petals, —

*Phœbe.*                              Old Ægidius

Belike had led thee there to gather flowers !

*Daphne.*   Yea, that may be.   And yet he trod
them down

As they were paupers plucking at his robe

To ask an alms.

*Phœbe.*            Who raileth at him now !

Did not the nervous flitting dragon-fly

Skurry away in fear his silver wings

Might tempt Ægidius' greed?

*Daphne.*                Nay, I let slip

A careless word ; but, sooth, I did not rail.

That is thine office.

*Phœbe.*          Nor will I be slow

Fulfilling it on old Ægidius.

When like a satyr he had trampled down —

As he would love ! — the brookside blooms,

What did he then ?

*Daphne.*        He pointed with his hand —

*Phœbe.*  His hungry hand, as lean as the brown

    rake

Gleaning stray ears along the harvest-field !

*Daphne.*  Mayhap ; he surely hath well har-

    vested.

He pointed with his jewel-freighted hand ; —

O girl, what woman could resist such gems ! —

He showed me all the fields beyond the brook,

The wavelike meadows and the olive groves,

And the far upland turning tawny gold

With coming harvest. " These are mine ! " he

    said.

Phœbe, and if I will, all these are mine !

*Phœbe.*    Ye gods, and is this Daphne ! I have set

My faith, yea, love itself upon thy truth.

Phaon, we are betrayed !

*Daphne.*                    Nay, foolish girl,

I am not bound to please thee in my choice.

Should I wed poverty to serve thy need?

Nay, look not so aghast !   All is not done ;

The die not cast.   Love plagues my bosom still ;

Who knows but that he yet may have his will !

(DAPHNE *embraces* PHŒBE, *and leads her out.*)


SCENE VII

*Enter* CREON, ÆGIDIUS, DAPHNE, PHŒBE, PHAON,

*and* STREPHON.

*Creon.*   Daphne, in virtue of my office here,

I must recall the vow which thou hast made.

By great Apollo's altar hast thou sworn

Now that the sacrifice is done to choose

Between Ægidius and unworthy me.

Art thou content, and wilt thou answer now?

*Daphne.*   I am content.

*Creon.*                    Ægidius, is there aught

Thou wouldst before the high gods say to her

Ere that she answer to her vow?

*Ægidius.*                    Daphne,

Already have I told thee many times

How dear I hold thee, and how great a price

I 'd pay to make thee mine, the dearest gem

Of all my precious hoards. Shouldst thou choose me,

I 'll set thy gilded marriage chains with gems

Till thou wilt flaunt them as rich ornaments,

Even in face of queens.   I am not young,

But every year have I at so great price

Sold unto Time that what I lack in youth

I can redeem with wealth a thousandfold.

Say but the word, and all I have is thine.

> *Strephon.*   Lives there a woman could resist such
>     bribe ?

Sure, Phœbe, thou art mine !

> *Phœbe.*                    Not yet !   Not yet !

> *Daphne.*   Creon, thou   hearest   what   Ægidius
>     gives ;

What canst thou offer to compete with this ?

> *Creon.*   Nothing ; unless that love may turn  the
>     scale.

If thou dost choose me, thou hast only me ;

If to have me is not to have the world,

Thou wilt have nothing, having only me.

If thou dost love me not, then choose me not.

I cannot gild thy chains.   I love thee so

I could not bear thee mine when thou wert mine

Only in name.   Rather than feel thy lip

Shrink at my kiss, — nay, not so much as shrink,

But fail to press eager to meet mine own, —

I would that I might never see thee more !

Love me with all thy heart, or pass me by.

   *Phaon.*   If she be woman, then his cause is won !

   *Daphne.*   Sir, for thy golden   offers have my

     thanks ; —

And yet thou offerest naught but golden chains !

Thou hast forgot to ask if I could love ;

And loveless wedlock is worst slavery.

I would not seem ungrateful, yet methinks

Thou hast mistook me for a thing on sale !

If I were so, I were not worth a price

So great as that thou profferest.   Creon, thou

Hast rather claimed than proffered, asking all,

No less than to my very soul's last thought.

Thou claimest all : my maiden self, my love,

My liberty ; that I should circumscribe

My present and my future to thy will ;

And ask from destiny naught but thy smile.

Well, — be it so; for love with woman is

To give, and give, and give.  I am all thine!

*Creon.*  Since all I am and all I have is thine,

To give to me is not to give, but keep.

*Phaon.*  Phœbe, thou art my wager, but I scorn

To hold a woman by constraint.

*Phœbe.*                              And I

To be constrained; so I am thine by will.

*Strephon.*  Ægidius, thou and I might hang our-

selves;

Little there seemeth else for us to do !

*Ægidius.*  What fools men be who say the Golden

Age

Is come again, if gold no more will buy

Beauty and love !  I give them all the lie !

*Creon.*  The Golden Age is come, since beauty

gives

Love unto love, and thus in beauty lives !

# THE LILIES OF MUMMEL SEE

# THE LILIES OF MUMMEL SEE

I

*A starlit night in the forest. Sir Albrecht, with his*
*henchmen, Dietrich and Heinrich, followed by men-*
*at-arms, riding through a gloomy wood path.*

*Albrecht.*

THICKER the forest grows. I scarce
can see
The stars that like the winking eyes
of elves

Peer through the tree-tops black.

*Dietrich.*             Deeper our path

Leads down through woodland ways spell-haunted.

*Heinrich.*                 Hist !

It is not wise to speak of things like these
So near the fay-enchanted Mummel See.

    *Albrecht.* Ha, Heinrich, dost thou fear the forest
        sprites ?

Would we might see the elfin band, or meet,
Madly careering on his crashing course,
The great wild huntsman.

*Heinrich.*               Sooth, I fear not man,

But more than man the boldest may not face.

    *Dietrich.* Why be afraid? Fear cannot alter fate.

    *Heinrich.* Yet only fools will tempt a fate to fall.

It is Midsummer Night, when all abroad

The elfin bands throughout the forest roam;

When spells are till the morning hour unloosed,

And evil-working spirits are set free.

    *Albrecht.* Hark! Is there sound of music in

      the wood,

Or only night-birds calling?

    *Heinrich.*               'T is the fays!

Cross yourselves quickly!

    *Albrecht.*               Nay, I fear them not.

Spirits that sing so sweet cannot be ill.


*The sound of voices is heard from the forest, grad-*
    *ually drawing nearer.*

    *Fays.* It is Midsummer Night,

      Now blithe each fay and sprite

        To join the dance is winging;

      Hark! Hark! How sweet and clear

      Their voices greet the ear,

        Like fairy bells tinklingly ringing!

*Dietrich.* Hear how the chorus rises ; the whole wood

Trembles with swelling murmurs musical.

*Woodnymphs.* We love the aisles of the forest
trees,
And the pattering rustle of leaves ;
We love the murmur of morning breeze,
As it laughs or sings or grieves ;
But best we love the airy flight
To seek the elves in summer night.
By leafy ways to meet them,
We haste to find and greet them.
Hark ! Hark !  We hear
Their joyous singing clear ;
The elfin band is near.

*Elves.*       Light as mote
In the beam,
As they float,
As they gleam,
Do they hasten to find us ;
If we tease them,
Yet we please them ;
Still they follow,
By hill and hollow,

In embraces to bind us.

Fleet! Fleet! They 're behind us!

*Albrecht.* Hear how the amorous spirits mock

the night!

Are these thy magic spells so full of dread?

*Heinrich.* In this enchanted wood even at love

I tremble. Often spells of deepest woe

Under its gracious seeming lie in wait.

*Albrecht.* Wherever passion sets its foaming cup

To my quick lip, I quaff, and have no fear.

*Woodnymphs.* From magic spell set free,

To·night the lilies fair

That sleep on Mummel See

Their own true forms shall wear.

Till morn shall break

They joyance take

In dance and revelry.

*Albrecht.* List! What is this the wood-sprites

tell?

What sing they of the lilies of the lake?

*Heinrich.* The lilies float upon the Mummel See,

White as the pearly teeth of thy betrothed

Whose hand to-morrow's sacred rites makes thine.

Once were they nymphs ranging the forest through,

70

Fantastic fleeting down its moonlit glades,

Or in warm, languid nights disporting fair

In its hid streams; but the Lake Spirit dread

Hath charmed them by his power.  They moveless

    sleep,

Save only for this night of all the year.

Now they awake, and like thin mists that whirl,

They dance upon the lake till morn arise.

*Elves.*   Hasten fleet, trampling feet,

      From the spell-haunted lake.

    Be not bold to behold

    How the lilies will wake !

*Dietrich.* The  spirits  answer us !  Sweet  Jesu,

    save !

*Albrecht.* Fearest thou too?  What is there we

    should dread,

Though we should watch their beauty in the dance ?

*Fays.* Fatal the beauty of the fair lily daughters !

    Deep dwells the Lake Spirit under black

      waters ;

      And his charm

      Worketh harm.

    The power of his spell is above them,

    That man may not see but to love them.

But all passion is vain ;

They will love not again ;

Since love would consume them like fire,

And for them one are death and desire.

*Albrecht.* No beauty with its magic do I fear.

My heart is with fair Gertrude where she sleeps

Dreaming of me, and listens in her sleep

To hear the warder from the tower call

Sight of our torches on the hills afar.

Safe may I look, guarded by thought of her,

Even on spell-wrought loveliness unharmed.

*Heinrich.* By all the holy saints, I pray thee ride

While yet we ride unscathed.

*Albrecht.*                         Nay, I will watch

To spy these dancing darlings of the lake.

*Fays.*     Beware the fatal charm !

Flee, ere it work thee harm !

Beware the mystic spell !

Flee, while yet all is well !

*Heinrich.* If not to us, list how the very air

Cries out in warning !   Get thee on thy way !

*Albrecht.* Trouble me not.   See how the broad
     lake spreads

Its level dusk, flecked with the lilies fair,

As white as winnowed wheat upon the wave,

Or as the stars had fallen from on high.

Come ; let us leave the horses, while we stand

Where we can hear the unseen wavelets lip

The lake's marge with their kisses amorous.

 *Dietrich.* Idle it were when thou hast chose thy
  course

To hold thee back ; yet evil will befall.

*They leave the horses with the men-at-arms, and go
  down to the shore of the lake.*

## II

*Sir Albrecht, with the two henchmen, standing on the
  borders of the lake ; the spirits calling unseen from
  the forest about them.*

 *Woodnymphs.* Cold, on the lake's cold breast,
  The lilies white are sleeping ;
  Lulled in their wave-rocked rest,
   Of dreams the secret keeping.

 *Elves.*   Yet in sleep
    See them weep
     Dewy tears ;
    In their dream
    Do they seem
     Thrilled with fears.

And they quiver like the river-shaken reeds;

And they tremble to dissemble joy that breeds!

*Fays.* Even in sleep they feel the midnight hour,

That comes to wake them with its magic power.

*All.* The hour is here! They wake! They wake!

The magic bands of sleep they break!

*Albrecht.* Body of God! A miracle is wrought!

Saints, have ye comeliness like this in heaven?

*Dietrich.* I pray thee, blaspheme not!

*Heinrich.*                    Save us, O saints!

*Albrecht.* Peace, fool! What beings can more

blessëd be

Than these bright damsels shimmering on the

lake?

*Woodnymphs.* See the lilies in ecstasy waking,

Their bodies of loveliness taking.

Till the first cock crow,

And the night is done;

Till the fair star show

That foretells the sun,

In the dance do they glance the lake over,

Now advance, now retreat, singing ever;

Springing fleet, as the bee to the clover,

Clinging sweet, who so quickly must sever.

*Albrecht.*   See how the lilies like to moonbeams
    dance,

While all the rippling waves enamored spring

To kiss the tempting softness of their feet.

Ah, tender feet !   Would I might kiss them too !

*Lilies.*    White gliding feet,

       That meet the tide,

     Light sliding fleet,

       To peep and hide, —

    Arms moonbeam white,

      That gleam and leap,

    Reflected bright

      Along the deep, —

   Bosoms of snow,

     And sweep of hair

   Flung to and fro

     On smooth necks bare

   In flow of gold, —

     Our charms behold !

Weaving in mystical measures

   Fantastic figures and wild ;

Hinting at uncounted treasures,

Calling to turbulent pleasures,

   Till the fond heart is beguiled ;

Swaying, and twining, and bending,

Dance we in circles unending.

*Albrecht.* They beckon there, these glorious
forms of light ;

Their wreathing arms and panting bosoms ripe

Make my blood quicken, and my breath come
thick !

*Dietrich.* I fear the fell wood-witches ! On thy
soul

I charge thee look no longer.

*Heinrich.*                          Sweet, my lord,

Are the enchantments of this sorcery,

But it is death to linger. Come away !

*Lilies.* Winding in mazes entrancing,

Mock we the stars with our eyes ;

Turning our magical dancing,

Pausing, retreating, advancing,

Light as the thistle-down flies.

*Albrecht.* Se'st thou the maid fairer than love's
first thought

That leads the train ? She draws my heart to
hers

As stars draw upward leaping tongues of flame.

*Fays.* Cover thine eyes, and flee !

Think how love waits for thee.

For the bridal board is spread,

And the bridal wine gleams red;

Decked is the nuptial bed.

Cover thine eyes, and flee!

*Albrecht.* There is no love save that which holds me here;

Now first I know the taste of its sweet cup!

*Woodnymphs.* Cover thine eyes, and flee!

Honor is reft from thee!

Shall thy troth be pledged in vain?

Shall thy passion cleanse the stain?

False once must false remain!

Cover thine eyes, and flee!

*Albrecht.* There is no honor save in love's high hest!

My love is here, and here my faith abides.

*Dietrich.* Oh, listen to the spirits of the air!

Noble and wise their counsel is.

*Heinrich.*                    Oh, turn!

Think on thy bride! Think on thy plighted vow!

*Albrecht.* Vex me no more! On your allegiance, back;

Lest my sword teach ye bitter reverence!

77

*Lilies.* Yield, yield to beauty's melting spell.

Are we not fair as word could tell?

When love is won is not all well?

*Albrecht.* I yield! I yield! O most transcendent maid,

Draw near, and let thy dear lips speak to me.

*The Lily Nymph.* Out of the heart of the waters,

Out of the black wave below,

Fairest of all the white daughters,

Bloomed I as pure as the snow.

And man may not see but to love me,

For the power of a spell is above me;

And will by my glances is slain.

But passion in vain reacheth after;

I flee, and I mock it with laughter,

Though hearts ache with turbulent pain,

Though hearts break with passion and pain.

*Albrecht.* List to me, maid divine! Madness
hath clutched

With gripping hand of fire my heart and soul!

Oh, bend to me! Stretch out thy flower-soft
hand

Like a white snow-flake fluttering down the air.

Let me but clasp thy fingers; lay a kiss

Upon their tips like birdlings in a nest ;

And feel the warm joy gushing in a flood

To fill me overflowing as rich wine

Brims bubbling to the top a hero's cup.

Then if I die, I shall at least have lived !

   *Lily Nymph.* Ah, mortal, entreating,

      I glide past thee fleeting ;

      To passion a stranger

       I draw my brief breath.

      To listen were danger ;

       To love thee were death.

   *Albrecht.* My arm shall fend thee from the stroke

     of doom.

My love is mightier than the spell of fate !

Oh, listen, listen, for I am distraught

With thy beguiling loveliness !   My life

Hangs doubtful on thy word !

   *Dietrich.*               Oh, madness fell,

That man should match his puny self with fate !

   *Albrecht.* O love, my lips are parching for the

     dew

Of thine assuaging kiss !   My bosom yearns

To feel thee nestle to my breast !   My arms

Strain after thee across the mocking flood !

At least a little nearer bend thy grace,

That thy dear, star-thrown shadow fall on me !

   *Lily Nymph.*  It cannot be ; ah, no ; ah, no !

   And yet how can I leave thee so ?

   *Woodnymphs.*  She nears him, the dance breaking,

   Her sisters pale forsaking.

   *Dietrich.*  See how the white witch of the lake
draws near !

His hands almost touch hers !

   *Heinrich.*              Call out to him !

Repeat a Pater Noster in his ear !

   *Dietrich.*  Nay, doom itself hath drugged his
drowsy sense.

That which is fated surely must befall.

   *Albrecht.*  Nearer, a little nearer, O fair sprite !

   *Lily Nymph.*  My heart, what is 't thou nearest ?

   *Albrecht.*  Closer, that I at least may kiss thy
hand !

   *Lily Nymph.*  My heart, what is 't thou fearest ?

   He draws me with his glances ;

   What power my will entrances ?

   *Lilies.*  Beware, beware, O fairest

   Of our fair band unbroken !

If mortal love thou sharest,

  Thy doom is surely spoken.

*Dietrich.*  Hark, how a rustling shivers through
  the reeds,

While hollow moanings echo down the wood!

*Heinrich.*  She bends to him; now has he caught
  her hand;

Now draws her close!  Woe to the waiting bride!

*Woodnymphs.*  He clasps her, with kisses

    Her virgin lips staining;

    In maddening blisses

    Breast unto breast straining.

    Oh, joy that denieth

    The doom that awaits!

    Oh, love that defieth

    The word of the fates!

*Albrecht.*  Dearest, oh, dearest one!  Now first I
  know

The taste of life to find its savor love!

I thought thy greeting kiss had been as cold

As moonlight on the snow, but with quick fire

It answers to my own.  Ah, dearest one,

How hast thou borrowed from the chilly lake

This glowing warmth that tingles in thy lip?

*Lily Nymph.* My heart is gold; from deeps
below

I have drawn up the warm earth's glow;

And in this moment to thy lips

My very life and being slips!

*Albrecht.* Is this the doom, that hearts should
break for joy!

III

*Elves.*　　　See! The star

Of the morn

There afar

Newly born.

See! It pales.

See! It fails.

Brothers, hear;

Day is near.

*Woodnymphs.* With the lisp of light leaves in
the morning breeze shaken,

Down the dim forest aisles see the gleaming dawn
waken;

Softest glow, faintest flush, as the lake-ripples
quicken

Till they die on the beach, in the sky wax and
thicken.

Fast the morning star fades like a pearl dropped
in wine,

As more near and more clear doth the coming day
shine.

For the night is at end, and the trembling leaves
shaken

Down the long forest aisles call the day to awaken.

*Lake Spirit.* Return, return, ye Lily Maidens;

Once more your snowy semblance take.

Again my spells with might enchain you,

That naught your charmèd sleep may break.

Once more my word hath power;

Now wakes the morning hour.

*Lilies.* Backward returning we hasten,

Back to our magical sleep;

Soon in the sunbeams will glisten

Cool, dewy tears where we weep.

Tears, and not dew, will impearl us;

Faint like a breath will arise,

Borne on the breeze of the daybreak,

Murmur of lingering sighs.

Ah, cruel doom that constrains us,

Drawing us backward again;

83

Mystical spell that enchains us,

    Pining in longing and pain.

*Lake Spirit.* Return, return, ye Lily Maidens,

    Unless the taint of love ye know.

Then blighted fall your beauty holy,

    Withered and stained your leaves of snow.

      Once more my spell hath power;

      This is the fated hour.

*Lily Nymph.* The doom! The doom! It falls

    upon me!

Ah, dear one, fend me from this harm!

From bliss to which thy love hath won me

    The Spirit draws me by his charm;

    Even from love draws with that charm.

*Albrecht.* Fear not! I feel that love must con-

    quer fate;

Love such as ours may laugh to scorn his spell.

*Lily Nymph.* The doom! The doom! I may

    not flee it.

    Ah, dear one, all our hope is vain.

    Thy face, alas, no more I see it!

    Heart's dearest, I for thee am slain!

*Albrecht.* Heart's dearest! Love! Sweet! Droop

    not so! Look up!

Oh, let not fall those lids that shut the light

From the world and my heart ! I cannot bear

The awful coldness of thy frozen face !

What chills thy lips, which but a moment since

Burned with a fire that kindled all my soul?

O loveliest one, look up, look up, and smile ;

The world is done if doom hath smitten thee !

> *Dietrich.* Look ! By God's wounds, she fadeth
>> from his arms

As a thin mist-wreath melts into the air !

> *Heinrich.* Where has she gone? Oh, Jesu !
>> Sorcery !

> *Albrecht.* Where art thou, oh thou fairest maid
>> of earth !

Let doom upon me work its cursëd spite,

But spare thy tender beauty, which might move

Most coward hearts to give up life for thee !

> *Fays.* See, where once more fair the lilies are
>> lying

> White on the lake in the soft growing day ;

> High o'er the trees soar the early birds flying ;

> Quick must the elfin hordes hasten away.

> *Woodnymphs.* But the fairest of the flowers
>> Floateth blasted on the lake.

85

Ah, what joy may still be ours

That we have no hearts to break!

*Albrecht.* Am I indeed alone, and is love done?

What then boots me this empty cup of life?

The wine is quaffed, and bitter are the lees.

*Dietrich.* How now, my lord, why are thy looks
so wild?

*Albrecht.* As one who wakens from a blessed
dream

So rich that all the gifts of earth seem poor,

So sweet that to its bliss all else is sad,

I stand here reft and lorn.   Ah, Lily Maid,

Who through my love hast vanished into death,

That great outward unknown that mocks man's
power,

Thou takest with thee all life had of worth.

*Dietrich.* Nay, act the man!   Remember now
thy bride.

Shake off this damnèd spell.   Mount; mount, and
flee.

*Albrecht.* How can I flee away from my own
heart,

Which lies within yon lily's withered cup?

86

*Heinrich.* Seize him, and bear him hence.  He
stands amazed.

Pour holy words !   The spell is on him still.

*Albrecht.*  I charge you on your peril, touch me
not !   I go

To search the deep for her I love.   Farewell !

*Dietrich.*  Help, Heinrich !   Hold him fast, or
all is lost !

*Albrecht.*  All, all is lost unless I find her there !

[*He leaps into the lake.*

*Heinrich.*  Down to the depths he plunges like a
stone.

*Dietrich.*  That which is written in the book of
fate

No mortal man may alter or gainsay.

# UNDER THE BEECH-TREE

# UNDER THE BEECH-TREE

*A grassy glade in the forest, set about with trees. In
the midst of the scene is a magnificent beech, on the
trunk of which is carved a large monogram with
elaborate ornaments. At the foot of the tree is
a rustic bench. Two peasant women, AGATHA
and MARTHA, sit here together. The time is early
afternoon in September.*

*Martha.*

SOOTH, gossip, it is good to sit and rest.

    *Agatha.* Ay, it is good; rest is the
        bread of age.

*Martha.* See, there is Thekla yonder in the glade,
Twirling her distaff with a wind of sighs.

    *Agatha.* Poor Thekla, she is like the wounded
        fawn
Hans brought home from the wood. Her wistful
        eyes,
Tearless themselves, make tears spring hot in mine.

    *Martha.* Why need she then love Max and
        slight my Fritz?
Alas, my son that I shall see no more!

*Agatha.* Nay, gossip, Fritz will safely come
again ;

There is a lucky mole beside his chin.

*Martha.* Nay, Agatha, the night before he
marched

I heard the bittern crying in the marsh

From moonrise to the dawn.   He will not come.

Oh, when the great make war, and count the cost,

They do not reckon in the broken hearts

Of us poor women.

*Agatha.*          Truly they forget

Those that at home are spinning, blind with tears.

*Martha.*  What is it, Agatha, to you or me

Whether Duke Max or Duchess Emeline

Lives in a palace somewhere all at ease

And calls upon our sons to shed their blood ?

*Agatha.*  O Martha, do not talk of it !   I smile,

And bear my port as bravely as I may,

But my heart aches as would my bosom ache

If some foul ruffian bruised it with his fist.

*Martha.*  If there were tidings it would somewhat help ;

But this long waiting kills.   When Fritz was born

There was a death-watch ticking in the wall.

I lay there in my pain, and thought him dead
Ere he saw light.

*Agatha.*　　　　　But when your bosom felt
His little mouth, so sweet and wet and warm,
Tug till he hurt you —

*Martha.*　　　　　Nay, good gossip, peace,
Or I shall weep ! My heart clings to my son
As moss to this our beech ; yet where is he ?

*Agatha.* And what of me ? Has not my good
　　　man gone
To fight for our Duke Max ? I wake at night
To hear the owl hoot from the hollow oak,
And cower to my lonely bed, and moan,
My heart so hot with pain it dries my tears !
Would God the secret of the Duke's high birth
Had never come to light.

*Martha.*　　　　　Or he had died,
When underneath this beech the gipsy witch
Left him to feed the wolves !

*Agatha.*　　　　　Yet was the babe
As sweet as milk. I mind how Berthold found
The fearless nursling lying on the moss,
Catching the sunbeams in his dimpled hands
And laughing to himself. A wolf on watch

93

Lurked in the thicket, and yet dared not harm.

The very beasts knew him for royal born.

 *Martha.* Wiser they were than men then; for he
  grew

As Berthold's foster-son, and played with Fritz

As if his veins watered with peasant blood;

Only that Fritz must serve him in their sports.

 *Agatha.* Yea, Fritz was e'er his loving slave.

 *Martha.*         And won

A slave's reward, — to lose his very love!

Poor lad! He worshiped Thekla since they two

Babbled with baby lips.

 *Agatha.*      Like brother still

Hath Thekla held him.

 *Martha.*      Like a sister still

Hath Thekla slighted him for one she loved

Not like a sister. Well, she hath her meed.

When once the gipsy's lips, blue-black with death,

Had gasped the secret of his birth, an end

There was of his old love. He threw it by

With his rough garb. Fie on such fickle faith!

Do women never know true love from false?

 *Agatha.* Alas, we women hail the love that
  comes

94

Snapping a master's whip; for that which bends

To do us service have we little heed.

But she will turn to Fritz.

*Martha.*                    Ah, who can tell

If Fritz be quick or dead ?   Oh, God, for word

How goes the battle that shall make Max duke

Or leave him naught !

*Agatha.*          Hist !   Surely some one comes.

HANS, *travel-stained, in torn uniform, comes quickly*

    *down the glade.*   AGATHA *rushes into his arms.*

Hans !   Hans !   Thank God, 't is Hans !

*Hans.*                    Thank God, sweet wife !

*Agatha.* Thou art not wounded ?

*Hans.*                    Nay, wife, I am whole.

*Martha.* Where is my Fritz ?

*Hans.*                I left him with the Duke.

*Martha.* How dared'st thou leave my boy?

*Agatha.*                    Nay, Martha, hear !

*Hans.* Martha, the Duke hath lost —

*Martha and Agatha.*                Hath lost ?

*Hans.*                        Yea, lost ;

His soldiers fled as midges flee from rain.

*Martha.* But Fritz would not forsake him, e'en

    for me.

95

*Hans.* They fled the field together.

*Agatha.*                              They are safe.

Fritz knows the wood-ways as the badger knows.

Deft as the fox, that sees a cobweb-film

At night, and hears the footstep of an elf,

He 'll thread the forest.

*Martha.*                         But is Fritz unhurt?

*Hans.* Unhurt he left the field ; but at his side

Casper was killed.

*Martha.*              Oh, his poor mother !   Nay,

You would not lie to me ?   My Fritz is dead !

I see it in your eyes !

*Hans.*                    Peace, peace, good dame.

I tell thee Fritz came through the fray unscathed.

We met them in the valley where the shrine

Blesses with  peace  the  way.   Our  young  Duke
        rode

A tall white horse, like that the angel rides

In the great window of the church.

*Martha.*                              And Fritz ?

*Hans.* Fritz was behind him in the second rank.

The first went down like grass before a scythe,

And the white horse was hurt below the neck.

My ears ring now, so humanly he shrieked !

*Agatha.* But Duke Max?

*Hans.* He went down; then sprang again;
And some one set him on another horse.
It must have pleased him that this one was red,
And could not show the blood.

*Martha.* Yet Fritz was safe?

*Hans.* Safe? Who was safe until the strife was
done?
A great red-bearded soldier thrust at him
So close I thought the sword had reached his heart;
But Duke Max smote the red-beard; cleft his head
Down to the very chin.

*Agatha.* And Fritz was saved!
Somewhat, dear Martha, love the Duke for that.

*Martha.* Oh, take me home! My knees shake
under me.
Mother of God, bring thou my son again,
Or let me die believing he will come!

*They lead her out. When they are gone* THEKLA
*comes slowly down the forest path, spinning on her
distaff. She sings sadly.*

*Thekla.* My sweetheart gave a crimson blossom;
It withered soon upon my bosom.

97

Ah, sign of sorrow !

On the morrow

My love another love had found.


My sweetheart gave a kiss so burning

That all my breast was filled with yearning.

Ah, false the token !

Vows soon broken

That fond kiss falsely sealed for me.


My sweetheart gave a crimson blossom ;

It faded soon upon my bosom.

Yet love remaineth !

Though sore it paineth,

I would not from its smart be free.


How can I spin and sing as if to-day

Were like all days that linger out the year?

How can all things be so unchanged, unmoved?

The thin leaves do not quiver ; careless birds

Chant on untroubled ; bright the sun as joy.

O beech-tree, you were once a nurse to him ;

Here like a flower dropped he lay a babe.

He loved you well, and when he loved me well, —

Indeed, indeed, he once did love me well ! —

He gave the record to your keeping, carved

Here on your rugged breast ; and yet to-day

When greedy death and ruin snatch at him

With claws blood-dripping, all your light leaves
    dance

As blithe as on the day when here his lips

Sealed mine his own forevermore.

How can I bear it ?   How should woman bear

To have life still go on when love is done ?

When to look backward is an agony ;

When to look forward is despair.   Ah, me !

I hold my memories like burning coals

Upon my naked palms ; yet would I live

Only to cherish them, and blow them up

To burn with fiercer flame.   O God, who made

The heart of woman, pity her !

*She goes to the tree, and presses her cheek to the
    carving.*

                    The knife

That carved this token on your bark, dear tree,

Was not so keen of edge, cut not so deep,

As love that graved his image on my heart !

*She turns from the tree, and begins again to twirl her*
*spindle.*

But life and toil go on though love be done.

MAX *and* FRITZ *appear, coming down the glade.*
MAX *is in rich garb,* FRITZ *in uniform. Both are*
*disordered and travel-stained. They come up be-*
*hind* THEKLA *unseen.*

*Max.* Thekla!

 *She turns quickly, and springs toward them.*

*Thekla.* O Max!  (*She recovers herself, and*
 *draws back.*)  But no; it is the Duke.
Thank heaven Your Highness hath escaped from
 harm.
But why here in the forest?  Victory
Loves not to hide; but beats the boasting drum
And blows the self-complacent trump.  Your
 Grace —

*Max.* Oh, taunt me not with talk of victory
And bygone titles!

*Thekla.*    True, Your Highness comes
With little state —

*Max.*    It is my all.  This beech
Which saw me once a helpless, hapless babe,

Sees me to-day a helpless, hapless man,

The dupe and scorn of fortune ; stripped of all,

Save of base life.

    *Thekla.*        Max ! Fritz ! Can this be true ?

    *Max.* We come here beaten men, weak fugitives,

To cower and tremble if a beech-leaf fall !

We flee before the Duchess Emeline.

Dress me in woman's weeds, and let me take

Thy distaff and thy spindle, I that run

Before a woman !

    *Fritz.*        Thekla, comfort him !

    *Thekla.* But where thine army?

    *Max.*            Where the boasting word

Of yestermorn? Both vanished into air.

Once was I Duke ; now am I scarce a man !

    *Thekla.* Nay, manhood is its own estate, nor rests

On chance of fortune's changing, school-girl whims.

    *Fritz.* Defeat is but the test of loyalty.

To us thou art not changed because the horde

Of gad-fly courtiers no more rings thee round.

    *Max.* Alas, would I were changed ! I still am he,

That shadow of a Duke who could not win
Even the dignity of death.

  *Fritz.*       Thou still
Art he who like a hero fought, who last,
And fighting still, forsook the wicked field.
Thekla, he saved me in the very gasp
Of rushing, hideous death.

  *Thekla.*      Oh, tell me all,
Moment by moment, how that battle drew
Its monstrous length along.

  *Max.*      What words could tell
That battle with its smoke and blood and flame;
Its thunders tearing at the throbbing ear;
Its cries that pierced the breast like jagged blades;
Its fear that gripped the heart and made it ache
As aches the frost-bit cheek in wintry blast!
The air was mingled blood and fire and din,
Till we seemed swimming in a crimson sea,
Half flame, half tumult, — choked and feared to
    drown,
Frantic with terror, and yet mad to kill!
We snuffed up blood, tasted it in the air,
Sick to the soul, yet greedy still for more.
We could have bit the foemen in the throat

And sucked their blood like wolves! We were

not men;

We were made fiends incarnate, drunk with blood!

*Thekla.* No more! No more! I shall forget

the cause,

In woman's foolish pity. Let me think

Only upon thy right for which men fought.

True loyalty is not with one blow slain;

Hacked limb from limb, it keeps some spark of

life.

Gather the scattered troops. Were I a man,

I'd make defeat a war-cry, so to win

Success from failure!

*Max.*                    But thou art not man

Nor I a duke. So let the dream go by.

Woman is ne'er so true as to a cause

Lost beyond hope. My brave Fritz, stay no more.

Haste to thy mother; she will have thee slain

A hundred ways ere thou canst cross the wood.

Tell her the war is done.

MAX *goes to the beech, and stands back to the others,*

*looking at the carving.* FRITZ *approaches* THEKLA.

*Fritz.*                    Thekla, be kind!

What hope is left save only in thy love?

*Thekla.* Nay, Fritz, be kind. Bring not the old
    pain back.

Would I could love thee, but it may not be.

*Fritz.* Ah, who could love me, having known his
    love?

I ask for nothing; only comfort him.

He hath lost all.

*Thekla.*          Not all, O faithful friend,

Since thy staunch heart is still his henchman true.

*She extends her hand. He kisses it respectfully, and
goes out, looking back at* MAX. THEKLA *regards*
MAX *a moment; then she turns away, and begins
to spin, singing.*

*Thekla.* My sweetheart gave a crimson blossom,
    It withered soon upon my bosom.

*Max (coming toward her).* Thekla! Thekla,
    thou hast not greeted me.

*Thekla.* I surely said: "Thank Heaven Your
    Grace is safe."

*Max.* Nay, that was greeting to that poor
    Duke Max

Who lives no longer, even whose thin wraith

Was exorcised in blood on yon red field.

Hast thou no word to give a luckless friend,

One who dare hardly call his shadow his?

    *Thekla.* If then thou art my friend, though I
        may be

No friend of thine, be welcome to our wood.

    *Max.* Ah, Thekla, once I did not need to beg

A greeting, nor was that I won so poor.

    *Thekla.* A greeting begged must be a beggar's
        dole.

    *Max.* Poor alms, half charity and half con-
        tempt!

Perchance it is my meed.

*She sits down on the bench; he hesitatingly follows
her. She sits spinning; he leans on the end of the
bench a moment, then sits.*

    *Thekla.*              Tell me the tale

Of all that hath befallen since the day

When came those great men with their wondrous
        word

To make thee duke. Our humble wood was
        filled

With knights gem-crusted ; conscious plumes out-
        waved

Our beeches and our rowans.   Our shy birds

Were silenced by the clear-voiced bugle's cry

Of merry impudence.   Bold pages, bright

As crocuses, made love to flattered maids,

Who blushed and giggled all the while they
　　glanced

Beneath their lashes, feigning to be coy.

A day we saw the show; and then the place

Was empty; we dull peasant folk were left,

Wide-eyed and giddy-pated at the thought

That we had known Your Highness unaware.

　　*Max.* Thekla, thou wert not wont to mock me
　　　　thus.

　　*Thekla.* Perchance I had not cause.   But to thy
　　　　tale.

Since spring with amber leaflets hung the beech

Much hath befallen that I fain would know.

　　*Max.* Would all might be forgot!   What
　　　　shall I tell?

My mind is like a heap of wind-vexed leaves,

And every memory is stained with shame.

Thou know'st already the wild tale they told,

How I was only son of the old Duke,

Stolen by gipsies, left here in the glade,

And heir instead of Duchess Emeline.

I rode with those shrewd courtiers, cat-sleek
    men,

Whose every glance was cunning thrice distilled ;

I knew they watched me with their shifty eyes,

Appraising me, — but thought they gauged my
    worth

To wear the crown.  Simple, besotted dolt !

They took the measure of their dupe and tool.

 *Thekla.*  I marked them as they rode, and knew
    them false.

 *Max.*  Would I had been so wise !  Too late I
    learned,

Finding myself a make-weight in their games,

Hardly a helpless something in their schemes !

The worst and wisest of them all was he,

The silver-bearded man with falcon eyes,

Who reined his steed that day under our beech,

And praised the carving ; while I thought, poor
    fool,

I went to shape a dukedom as I graved

Our letters here.  Upon my soul I think

His crafty head divined that I had cut,

And so he tolled me with cheap flattery.

*Both turn to look at the carving. Their eyes meet,
and they look away in confusion.* THEKLA *takes
quickly the spindle in her lap, and begins again to
spin.*

*Thekla.* Yea, I remember; for I stood beside,
And felt as if he took my heart, and laughed,
Holding it up for all the world to gaze.
Cruel and cunning must that old man be.

    *Max.* Sooth, he — Godmar — is shrewder than
      a fox.
His right hand cheats his left; his fulsome
      tongue
Beguiles its very self with flattery.
Yet somewhere in his wise head lurks a will
That shapes whatever right or left hand do,
Whatever tongue may say or brain may think,
Bending it all to service of his craft.
Faugh! How he moulded me with cunning
      talk,
Shaping me to his wish the while he seemed,
More pliant than a reed, only to bend
As I was breeze to blow! My soul is sick
To think how he befooled!

    *Thekla.*          Nay, how hadst thou

The guile to match his art? How shouldst thou

 have?

Here in the wood we learn not knavery.

 *Max.* He blew about me hints as light as down,

That like to down stuck fast. Now would he note

The duty of a ruler, who must wed

To fix his power and render place secure;

Then of a young man's loneliness whom fate

Set unwed on that empty height, a throne;

Anon would praise the beauty and the grace,

The wit, the warmth, the woman's every charm,

Of Emeline —

 *Thekla.* The Duchess Emeline?

 *Max.* Yea, the great Duchess; and I own her fair

As a white fountain springing in the sun.

Godmar would have us wed —

 *Thekla.* Thou art not wed?

 *Max.* That when my right was welded to her

 claim

Our throne might stand unshaken. Once our

 hands

The priest had joined —

 *Thekla.* Nay, Max, thou art not wed?

How can be hers the heart that once was mine?

*Max.* Of hearts it mattered not. When great
ones match

Love is not bidden to the festival.

The Duchess feared my claim, and when we met

She found me not unroyal in my mien.

*Thekla.* Thou hast forgot that once we loved;
that here,

Sworn each to love the other e'en through death,

Under a new-born moon we said good-by.

*Max.* Ah, would that moon had never pricked
the clouds

Of mulberry-tinted eve !

*Thekla.*                     Since thou art wed —

*Max.* Nay, sweet, if in the wood I learned not
guile,

At least I learned of love, and had no mind

To wed unloving.  Think'st thou I forgot

The golden hours when I might kiss thine hair,

Thy brow, thy very lips; when thou wouldst
rest —

*Thekla.* I pray thee, peace! Have pity! Can
I bear

The shame of memories like these ? Tell on;

Only not this I know but all too well.

*Max.* When Godmar brought me face to face at last

With her whose throne I claimed, softly she smiled,

As one smiles at some pleasant inner thought,

The while her glances searched me through and through.

"Cousin," she said, "for such they say thou art,

Why need we war, and set on hapless men

To kill each other to decide our cause,

When we may make it one?" "How may that be?"

I questioned, though I feared what she must mean.

The red flushed in her cheeks as up the sky

The earliest hint of dawn comes in the cool.

"If we were one," she murmured, "then our cause

Were not divided." How my foolish heart

Beat like a hare's entrapped, man though I was!

    *Thekla.* And she is beautiful, and wooed thee thus?

    *Max.* She was so lovely and so womanly;

So winning yet commanding as she stood,

Hardly could I resist. Love stirs the heart

Though unrequited; and her eyes spoke love.

*Thekla.* What didst thou answer her? What couldst thou say?

*Max.* "Cousin," I said, " — I thank thee for the name, —

It might be better if this thing could be;

But how could we be one when my poor heart

Is left there in the forest whence I came?"

*Thekla.* Thou saidest that?

*Max.*　　　　　Nay, the words said themselves.

Something within me spoke, some inner self

That could not brook that love should be defamed.

*Thekla.* Ah, poor dead love! Wert thou so true to that

Which thine own hand had slain? What said she then?

*Max.* Then all her softness hardened as the pool

Skims with black ice beneath the touch of frost.

"Then is it war," she breathed; "the fault not mine!"

Old Godmar cursed me in his beard frost-white

As if with sanctity, — a nest of lies!

Through me he thought to rule her curbless pride,

Which without me for bridle mocked his hand.

And so we fought; and so, forsooth, I lost.

*Thekla.* Is it for crown or Duchess lost — that

    sigh ?

*Max.* Perchance for both; yet neither I re-

    gret ;

Though I could weep for the old, simple days,

When I was still a happy forester.

    *He rises from his seat, and walks to and fro.*

How in the palace longed I for the wood,

The never-ended laughter of its leaves,

Its twinkling smiles of sunshine flashing joy,

Its cool, green privacies of tender shade

Where dove-eyed peace dwells in the silences.

My nostrils hungered for the wholesome scents,

The odor of the pines, the smell of buds

Or moss new-wet with rain.  I could not breathe

In those great chambers filled with breath of men

A thousand times used over, thick with lies.

I stifled for the clean air of the wild !

    *Thekla.* And I here in the wood hated each

      glade,

Each secret forest path where thou and I,

Spattered with moonlight fallen through the trees

Like showers of gold-dust flung by tricksy elves,

Wandered together.  When the bold sun came,

And all the dewy mead laughed like a girl

With tears still on her cheeks, who sees her love

Late come at last, I looked out to the morn,

Cheating once more my silly, aching heart,

Saying : " To-day, ah, sure to-day it is

That he will send some smallest word ! " I saw

The amber leaflets on the beech grow green,

The springing grain wax tall, till in the heat

The shrill cicadas called the harvesters,

Chiding delay ; and I, who could not call,

Waited in silence ; yet thou didst not come !

    *Max.* Ah, what excuse can justify my love ?

    *Thekla.* The love that needs excuses is not love.

MAX *pauses a moment in silence.  Then he walks
away and returns.*

    *Max.* Thekla, I cast away thy love, nor dare,

So proved unworthy, ask that gift again ;

Yet wouldst thou be at least my friend once more,

Though I am fugitive, and dogged by scorn —

THEKLA *rises quickly and comes to him.  As her eyes
meet his her glance falters.  She turns away, and
begins nervously to twirl her spindle.*

*Thekla.* The woman who has loved no more en-
dures

Pale friendship, thin and cold. I loved thee
once ;

I may not be thy friend.

*Max.* So be it then.

Not twice doth Fortune offer man her best.

Lo, I let fall her gift, and won her scorn.

Farewell, since nothing thou of me wilt take

Save this poor word. Now I no more may set

My lips up to thy nestling mouth, I lay

A kiss here on thy name, as one might press

Remembrance on a dead, responseless brow.

*He goes to the tree, and kisses the carving. Then he
turns toward her.*

Farewell.

*Thekla.* Farewell ? Max ! Whither dost thou
go ?

*Max.* What doth it matter, since no more for
me

Life holds or good or hope ? I cast love by,

Yet could not for a crown that love forswear.

So love and crown together slip away.

Yet thou hast loved me ! Naught can alter that !

*He goes down a forest path, disappearing at the back.*

THEKLA *extends her hands to him, but he does not see. She stands thus until he is gone.*

*Thekla.* Oh, blind to see not that I love thee still!

Max! Max! Return!

*Enter* FRITZ *hastily.*

*Fritz.* Where hath His Highness gone?
Godmar is come, and fumes to find him not.
Disastrous were delay.

*Thekla.* Godmar is come!
What makes he here?

*Fritz.* The Duchess sends by him
Proffers of amity. She would have peace
Rung in with bridal bells.

*Thekla.* Now comes the proof
Shall try him to the quick!

*Reënter* MAX.

*Max.* Didst thou not call?
Fritz, art thou here?

*Fritz.* Yea, and thou still art Duke.
Godmar is here with message from Her Grace,
Who prays thee come to her.

*Thekla.* She loves thee still!

116

*Max.* She knows her state more stable if she
    wed
Her power to my right.   I will not go.

       GODMAR *comes fiercely down the glade.*

*Godmar.* Why dost thou linger here? A wo-
    man's moods
Run forward like the clock, and must be caught
Upon the prick of time or they are gone.
Come while to-day thy Duchess loves thee well ;
For who can tell how soon her whim may change.
To-morrow knows no love of yesterday.

    *Thekla.* If she can change, then hath she never
    loved !

    *Max.* Thekla, thou hast not changed! Thou
    lov'st me still !

       *He takes her hands.*

Go, Godmar ; with the Duchess make thy peace,
Saying the abdication of my right
Thou hast wrung hardly from my fear.   Thekla,
With thee here in the wood !

    *Godmar.*           Nay, thou art spoiled
For the old life.   When the first courtier bent,
His homage changed thee from a forester.
Since thou hast tasted princes' fare, no more

The black bread of the peasant suits thy taste.

The savor of thy by-gone royalty

Will taint the collops of fresh venison,

And make the woodland ale tang flat and thin.

Mistress, why silent? Didst thou truly love,

Thou wouldst persuade him from this madness.

> *Thekla.*                                        I!

> *Godmar.* Ay, thou! He boasted thy unselfish
> faith

E'en to the Duchess, who with eager hands

Proffered him crown and self. Make good his
> words!

> *Thekla.* I love him, sir, so that my very life

I would lay down to win him happiness.

Yea, more than life I would lay down, — my love!

> *Godmar.* Prove then thy love. Persuade him
> that he take

A nobler mate, and see thy face no more!

> *Max.* The worth of love is counted not by
> blood;

No mate out-toppeth her!

> *Fritz.*                                What must she say?

> *Thekla.* Max, all the future hangs upon thy
> choice.

Here in the forest wilt thou not regret

The splendor of the state thou dost forego?

Tossing on pallet hard wouldst thou not sigh

For couch of down where dreams of pomp and

    power

Rustle from silken curtains? When the wood

Is winnowed by the huntsman's eager horn,

And gay thy former courtiers pass thee by

With caps undoffed —

*Max.*            Nay, if thou lovest me

Let all the world go by. I heed it not.

    *Godmar.* This is the madness of a love-sick

        fool!

    *Fritz.* 'T is wiser than thy wisdom!

    *Thekla.*            Hear me still.

If time should come a son climbs on thy knees,

And with his baby fingers moulds thine heart,

Couldst thou yet be content, even for him?

Wouldst thou not mourn that for his golden hair

Thou hadst no crown, — for him, thy dearer self?

    *Godmar.* Would thou wert Duchess!

    *Max.*           Godmar, thou hast said!

What were thy Duchess in exchange for this?

Once have I been befooled. I fall not twice.

Thekla, if Fate that gives thee back to me,

Grant that I look in the compelling eyes

Of thy sweet son and mine, I shall not shrink

Knowing he hath no wealth but honest toil;

But count him richer than a hundred kings

In that thou art his mother!

MAX and THEKLA embrace.

Fritz.                    All is said!

Thekla. (drawing away from MAX). Alas, not

  yet! Dear Max, I needs must say

The word that parts us, though our constant hearts,

Like sound and echo answer each to each

Across the space between.

Max.                    We cannot part!

Thekla. Till death I keep remembrance of the

  glow

My bosom felt on thine in this glad hour;

Thy kiss not even death plucks from my lips.

  Max. But I will plant unnumbered kisses there!

  Thekla. Nay, dearest, thou and I no more are

  one.

Thou art our Duke. — Yet not for all thy state

Canst win such faith as thou dost leave behind!

Nor could thy crown, nor power of proudest kings,

Offer me boon of preciousness like this,

That I have proved thy love, and know it mine.

Go ; wed thy Duchess.   Now my heart can bear

Even that thou shouldst love her.

   *Max.*                        Nay, sweet, hear !

   *Godmar.* By  heaven,  thou  forest  girl,  thou

        shouldst be queen !

Thekla, for sake of thee, I, who have sought

Only to make him puppet to my will,

Will guide him for his good.   He shall not fail

To prove him worthy of thy sacrifice.

   *Max.* I will not give thee up !

   *Thekla.*                  I am not thine.

I was the forester's ; never the Duke's.

Dear heart, not only for ourselves we live.

The farthest star that twinkles down the night

Moves not alone, but is a chorister

Whose  voice  must  fail  not  in  heaven's  choiring

        host ;

The weed-bloom in the grass fulfills its part ;

Shall we fall from the worth of weed and star ?

Ah, would that we two — only thou and I —

Were set in some lone isle, by foam-fanged waves

Guarded forever from the world of men,

Where love should be our only bound and law !

   *Max.* Let us flee thither !

   *Thekla.*                   Nay, it may not be.

Who flees from duty never wins to rest.

How could we drown remembrance thou hadst cast

Thy heritage away ; that we had robbed

Thy people of their lord, thine unborn son,

Defenseless, of his birthright.

   *Max.*                  Listen, sweet, —

   *Thekla.* Nay, since this must be, make it not
      more hard,

Lest I give way ; — I am a woman still ! —

And all my life be seared with grief and shame

That when my love's proof was to give thee up,

And keep thee worthy of that love I failed.

Sir (*to* GODMAR), I have cursed thee in my heart
      ere this,

But now my beads shall daily know thy name

Murmured to heaven with his.   Fritz, love to us

Comes with veiled face, yet may it be he leads

Upward toward heights serene.   O Max, be sure

It is more blessed to have known thy love,

Even to lose, than to have won the world !

*She turns, and walks toward the forest. As she*
*passes the beech, she kisses the carving. As she*
*goes,* GODMAR *uncovers, and stands respectfully*
*until she disappears.*

*Max (starting forward).* Stay, sweetheart!
Stay!

*Godmar (restraining him).* Nay, trouble not her
peace.

Our way is to the world of lesser men.

123